MW01452040

CLASSIC
StoryTellers

MATT CHRISTOPHER

Mitchell Lane PUBLISHERS

P.O. Box 196
Hockessin, Delaware 19707

Titles in the Series

Beverly Cleary

E. B. White

Edgar Allan Poe

Ernest Hemingway

F. Scott Fitzgerald

Harriet Beecher Stowe

Jack London

Jacqueline Woodson

John Steinbeck

Judy Blume

Katherine Paterson

Mark Twain

Matt Christopher

Mildred Taylor

Nathaniel Hawthorne

Ray Bradbury

Stephen Crane

CLASSIC
StoryTellers

MATT CHRISTOPHER

Kathleen Tracy

Mitchell Lane
PUBLISHERS

Copyright © 2009 by Mitchell Lane Publishers, Inc. All rights reserved. No part of this book may be reproduced without written permission from the publisher. Printed and bound in the United States of America.

Printing   1   2   3   4   5   6   7   8   9

Library of Congress Cataloging-in-Publication Data
   Tracy, Kathleen.
     Matt Christopher / by Kathleen Tracy.
   p. cm. — (Classic storytellers)
   Includes bibliographical references (p.   ) and index.
   ISBN 978-1-58415-535-5 (lib. bdg.)
   1. Christopher, Matt—Juvenile literature. 2. Sportswriters—United States—Biography—Juvenile literature. 3. Authors, American—20th century—Biography—Juvenile literature. 4. Children's literature, American—Authorship—Juvenile literature. I. Title.
GV742.42.C48T73 2007
070.4'49796092—dc22
[B]   2007000667

ABOUT THE AUTHOR: Kathleen Tracy has been a journalist for over twenty years. Her writing has been featured in magazines including *The Toronto Star's Star Week*, *A&E Biography* magazine, *KidScreen* and *Variety*. She is also the author of numerous biographies and other nonfiction books, including *Judy Blume*, *Mariano Guadalupe Vallejo*, *William Hewlett: Pioneer of the Computer Age*, *The Watergate Scandal*, *The Life and Times of Cicero*, *Mariah Carey*, *Kelly Clarkson*, *Aly and AJ*, *Johnny Depp*, and *The Plymouth Colony: The Pilgrims Settle in New England* for Mitchell Lane Publishers. She divides her time between homes in Studio City and Palm Springs, California.

SPECIAL THANKS to Dale and Duane Christopher and Andrew Johnston of Louise Pettus Archives and Special Collections at Winthrop University for all their help with this book. This story has been reviewed and approved for print by Dale and Duane Christopher.

PUBLISHER'S NOTE: This story is based on the author's extensive research, which she believes to be accurate. Documentation of such research is contained on page 46.
    The internet sites referenced herein were active as of the publication date. Due to the fleeting nature of some websites, we cannot guarantee they will all be active when you are reading this book.

PLB

Contents

MATT CHRISTOPHER
Kathleen Tracy

Chapter 1	Early Influences 7
	*FYInfo: General Electric 11
Chapter 2	Humble Beginnings 13
	FYInfo: Lou Gehrig 19
Chapter 3	Baseball Calls 21
	FYInfo: John J. McGraw 27
Chapter 4	The Lucky Baseball Bat 29
	FYInfo: Pulp Magazines 35
Chapter 5	A Lasting Impact 37
	FYInfo: Typewriters 42

Chronology 43
Selected Works 43
Timeline in History 44
Chapter Notes 44
Further Reading 46
        For Young Adults 46
        Works Consulted 46
        On the Internet 46
Glossary 47
Index 48

*For Your Information

When Matt was 12, his family lived in an old and run-down house—that was said to be haunted! For the rest of his life, Matt would have an interest in mysteries and suspense stories because of his experiences in the family's haunted home.

Chapter 1

EARLY INFLUENCES

When he was 12 years old, Matt Christopher's family moved to the small town of Portland Point, New York. It was the fourth time they had moved since he was born, and the second time they had lived in Portland Point. But this move was very different from the others. This time the Christophers were moving into a haunted house.

According to the local gossip, the house Matt's family would call home had been the scene of a murder 20 years earlier. Since then, people in the neighborhood had reported seeing an otherworldly apparition hovering in and around the house.

To most people, the property certainly looked like something out of a horror film. According to Dale Christopher's biography of his father, "The house had been vacant and neglected for several years. The boards of the steps leading up to the porch were buckled and rickety. A single wooden chair sat next to the front entry. The screen door hung from the top hinge only. The screen itself was ripped at one corner and flapped every time the door moved.

Chapter 1 EARLY INFLUENCES

"Inside, the house was just as run-down."[1]

Despite how the house looked, Matt wasn't scared. After walking around his new home, he decided it simply needed a family to bring it to life. While Matt's dad and grandfather, who lived with them, spent the day working at the local cement plant, his mother worked just as hard to fix up the house. Although they didn't have a lot of money, they were happy just being together as a family and felt comfortable in their new home. None of the Christophers believed for a moment their happy house was haunted.

That was about to change.

One night Matt was sound asleep in the bedroom he shared with his brothers on the second floor. His grandfather's room was also upstairs. Suddenly, Matt and his brothers were jolted awake by a terrified yelp. They listened as somebody ran down the stairs in a mad dash.

Matt and his brothers bolted out of bed and ran downstairs. Their parents and sister had also heard the commotion and had come out of their rooms to see what was going on. They found Matt's grandfather in the kitchen, looking as if . . . well, as if he'd seen a ghost. Still clearly upset, he nervously told Matt's dad what had happened—in Italian. Mr. Christopher translated for his family.

"He said somebody pulled the blanket off of him . . . ," Matt recalled. "And then this somebody began to shake the bed. But when he turned on the light, nobody was there."[2]

What scared Matt the most was seeing his father frightened by what had happened. Had it been an intruder? Had his grandfather been dreaming? Was it really a ghost? It was a mystery that was never clearly solved. Although there were no more incidents after that, nobody ever felt completely at ease in the house again. A year later, the Christophers moved to a different home, grateful to be leaving the haunted house behind.

Ironically, the experience spurred Matt's interest in mystery and suspense stories. Years later, when he was struggling to establish himself as a professional writer, he decided to author a mystery book. Before starting, he read as many mysteries as possible, both for inspiration and to learn how mystery writers craft their stories. After he came up with an idea he liked for his own book, he carefully worked out the plot and developed the characters. Finally, he was ready to start writing. Because he had a full-time day job, he could work on his book only during his lunch hour and at night.

It took Matt a year to finish that mystery, which he called *Lay the Body Anywhere*. It was his first full-length book.

Writing it was only half the work. Now he had to try to get it published. Up to then, Matt had written nothing but short stories for magazines. In those cases, he had simply mailed the stories directly to the magazines. But book publishers had different procedures. If he wanted editors to read his novel, Matt needed an agent to act as his representative.

The agent Matt contacted agreed to represent him, but only if Matt made some revisions to the manuscript—and also sent $50 for the agent's assistance in revising. It was money Matt really couldn't afford—by then he was married with children and struggling financially—but he sent it anyway.

While waiting to hear from the agent again, Matt and his wife were forced to sell their home and move to a new city. They bought a large building that had two apartments upstairs and space for two businesses downstairs. The plan was to make enough money renting out the extra apartment and office space so that Matt could write full-time.

Still no word from the agent. For the next two years, Matt kept writing short stories, but he didn't try writing another book. Why bother when all that work had been for nothing?

Realizing he was not making enough money as a writer to support his family, Matt looked for other work. A job as a door-to-door salesman lasted only a couple of weeks before he quit. He was hired to drive a laundry truck, which paid well, but the hours were so long Matt was too exhausted to write. It began to look as though his chance to be a professional writer had come and gone.

Through one of his laundry customers, Matt got a job on the television assembly line at the local General Electric plant. The work

Chapter **1** EARLY INFLUENCES

To support his wife and children, Matt (center) worked at the local General Electric plant. He eventually quit when he felt he was unfairly passed over for a promotion.

was easy, and Matt had enough energy when he got home to tackle his stories. Even if he couldn't make a living at it, Matt continued to write because it was truly his passion.

Finally, Matt heard from his agent. He opened the letter and was shocked to read that his novel had been sold. The publisher, Phoenix Press, had retitled the book *Look for the Body* and paid him an advance of $150.

That was the only money the book would make. Even though his first novel was a commercial failure, being published gave Matt the encouragement he needed to keep writing. He would try several more times to break into the mystery genre, but the books just didn't generate any interest.

Rather than get discouraged, Matt took each rejection as a learning experience. Just as he had faced the prospect of moving into a haunted house with optimism, he was convinced his big break was within reach. He simply needed to find the right readers for his stories. When he did, those readers would be a completely unexpected audience.

FYInfo

General Electric

Thomas Edison wasn't just a brilliant inventor; he was also an extremely successful businessman. After Edison invented the first affordable, efficient incandescent lightbulb in 1879, he foresaw the huge potential of the new technology and spent the following years establishing America's electric industry.

On September 4, 1882, the first commercial power station began generating electricity. Located on Pearl Street in Manhattan, the station provided power to 59 customers located within a one-mile radius. Suddenly, people had a way to get electricity 24 hours a day at an affordable price. By the end of the decade, power stations were being built in cities all across America.

Edison wasn't the only entrepreneur trying to profit from the country's growing demand for energy. In 1879, Elihu Thomson and Edwin Houston had formed the Thomson-Houston Electric Company, which was a direct competitor to Edison General Electric. As the industry grew it became clear that the two companies would be more successful by joining forces, so in 1892, they merged to form the General Electric Company, also known as GE. Although Edison never actually controlled his companies, he became a millionaire from his inventions and earned worldwide fame as one of the most influential inventors in modern history.

Thomas Edison's first lightbulb, used to demonstrate his invention at Menlo Park

By the time Matt Christopher went to work at General Electric in the 1940s, he was joining one of the most successful and diverse companies in America. In 2000, *Forbes* magazine listed General Electric as the world's second-largest company, with over $152 *billion* in sales annually. It also became the third-largest media conglomerate in the world, owning the NBC television network and Universal Studios—appropriate, since Edison's invention of the motion-picture camera paved the way for Hollywood's entertainment industry.

To fit in better, Matt's father Frederick changed the family name from Cristoforo to Christopher after he emigrated from Italy to the United States. The eldest of nine children, Matt (above) was expected to help with chores. As a result, he developed a strong work ethic that would prove invaluable later in his life.

Chapter 2

HUMBLE BEGINNINGS

Like many Americans of Matt's generation, the Christopher family immigrated to America from Europe looking for a better way of life. His father, Frederick Cristoforo, was born in Italy. When Frederick was ten years old, he came to the United States with his dad, Matteo, and an uncle. To fit in better in their new country, they changed their last name to Christopher and went to work at a cement plant in Bath, Pennsylvania. Even young Frederick was expected to hold down a job.

The area where they settled was located in mining country, and most of their neighbors were just as poor as they were. While living in Bath, Frederick met and fell in love with Mary Rose Vass, who had moved with her parents to the United States from Hungary. Like the Christophers, the Vasses were willing to work as hard as necessary to support themselves and be contributing members of American society. It was a work ethic that Frederick and Mary Rose would later pass down to their children.

Chapter 2   HUMBLE BEGINNINGS

The young couple married in 1916. A year later, their first child, Matthew, was born on August 16. He was named after his grandfather Matteo.

When Matt was a toddler, Frederick moved the family to the nearby town of Bath-Portland to be closer to the cement plant where both he and Matteo worked. Mary stayed at home, working hard to keep the house clean and care for their children. Between 1919 and 1924, Mary had three more children: Mary, Frederick Jr., and Michael. Eventually, she and Frederick would have five more children. Matt would later marvel at his mother's commitment to her family.

"I was the oldest of nine children—seven boys and two girls. It was quite an experience. Looking back now I don't know how my mother could do it. . . . I know that it was very troublesome for my mom to make breakfast, lunch, and dinner for nine children. Another thing is too, my grandfather was living with us. . . . So it was no easy thing. But as I recall now I don't think that bothered me that much. Of course [my mother] had problems all the way through, obviously, because she died of a heart attack before she was 52 years old."[1]

All the children were expected to pitch in with the chores. One of Matt's duties was to tend the garden located behind their house. In the 1920s, there were no well-stocked grocery stores where people could shop—and even if there had been, most of the families in Bath-Portland would not have been able to afford to do so. If families wanted to eat fresh fruits and vegetables, they grew them themselves. Because they worked long, hard hours doing physical labor, people burned a lot of calories. They needed foods high in carbohydrates, for energy, so potatoes and corn were the main vegetables grown in most family gardens every spring and summer. What they didn't eat right away was canned and stored in cellars to eat during the winter.

In 1925, the Christophers moved to Portland Point, New York. Within the year they moved again, this time to the city of Trenton, New Jersey, a major manufacturing center for steel, rubber, wire, rope, linoleum, and ceramics. Because it was an industrial city with plenty of jobs, 50 percent of those living in Trenton were immigrants, according to a 1920 census.[2]

MATT CHRISTOPHER

Matt attended first and second grade at a small schoolhouse in rural Bath-Portland, Pennsylvania. Today, Bath-Portland is known as Jacksonville.

    Unlike the smaller towns where the Christophers had lived, Trenton was a big city, with apartment buildings crammed together on narrow streets. After a couple of years, Frederick packed up his family one more time and returned to Portland Point. He and Matteo were rehired at the cement plant, and they moved into the haunted house, which was situated near a quarry. The home was constantly filled with dust from the workers' excavation blasts.

    Even though there were lots of chores to do, Matt and his siblings still found time to play. Baseball was by far Matt's favorite pastime. Since there was no baseball field in the area, the neighborhood kids improvised. According to Matt's son Dale:

Chapter 2   HUMBLE BEGINNINGS

The area behind Matt's house was the most open, so that's where they played. Their backstop was a woodshed built next to the Christophers' kitchen door. Flat stones were used for bases. The pitcher's mound was just a small hole in the ground. The batter's box was a square of dirt made by countless feet 'digging in' before each pitch. . . . Teams were usually short a few players, and since most kids wanted to play an infield position, there was always a hole in the outfield. None of the players could afford a real baseball bat, so they used a broom handle with tape around the grip to make it look like a major league bat. And since no one had a real baseball either, they used a worn tennis ball.[3]

Nobody had enough money to buy a real baseball mitt, so they used whatever they could find to protect their hands. Matt used cloth-covered cardboard.

The games would last as long as the boys were allowed to stay out, and these were some of the best times of Matt's youth. Years later, he would use many of his experiences playing sandlot baseball, and the boys he played with and against, as the inspiration for stories he wrote. But at the time, being a writer hadn't crossed his mind yet. Sports were his sole passion.

When he was a sophomore at Ludlowville High School, Matt earned a spot on the school baseball team. Getting to play in an official league made him fall in love with the sport even more. He soon began dreaming of being a professional ballplayer. Naturally athletic, Matt also played on the high school football team and enjoyed playing pickup basketball games with friends. Even though he could have happily spent all his waking hours playing sports, Matt also felt a responsibility to help his family financially.

When he was 14, Matt got a job selling magazine subscriptions. It was tedious work and not many people bought from him. But Matt enjoyed the job because he was able to read all the magazines he was supposed to be selling.

"We had parents from another country who couldn't read or write," Matt's brother John recalled in the *New York Times*. "We did not subscribe to magazines or a newspaper. There was no literature in the home. And yet here's a guy who gets excited about reading and writing. None of us were excited."[4]

For Matt, the experience exposed him to a new world—and a new passion. "I was selling magazines such as the *Saturday Evening Post, Country Gentleman*, and *Liberty*, and I would read the stories, particularly the adventure and mystery stories, and think how wonderful it would be to be able to write stories and make a living at it. I also read detective, horror, aviation, and sports stories and decided I would try writing them myself."[5]

Before he could send stories in to magazines, Matt needed a typewriter. Frederick didn't have the money to spend on such a luxury, but he bought his son an $18 Barr-Morse typewriter anyway. He obviously supported Matt's desire to write, but Frederick's real dream was to see him become a professional baseball player.

Baseball is known as America's pastime, and that was never truer than in the early 1930s. The Great Depression had started and people everywhere fell on hard times. As companies shut down, people lost their jobs and were unable to find new ones. Hunger was rampant. Families who lost their homes were forced to live in their cars, if they were lucky enough to have one, or in fields.

Therefore, baseball was not just a pastime but a much-needed diversion from the grim realities of daily life. Baseball players such as Babe Ruth, Lou Gehrig, Tony Lazzeri, Lefty O'Doul, and Rogers Hornsby were revered. Frederick genuinely believed Matt was good enough to turn pro; he also knew that the family could desperately use the money Matt would receive for signing with a pro team.

In 1934, the cement plant shut down, but Frederick and Matteo luckily found other jobs working with a construction crew. Matt also got a job with the crew, bringing water for the men to drink. It was hot, grueling work, but Matt never complained, seeing how hard his father and grandfather were also working to support the family.

Chapter 2   HUMBLE BEGINNINGS

Matt's parents worked hard to support their nine children. His mother, Mary Rose, suffered from ongoing health problems and died of a heart attack when she was just 51 years old. Frederick eventually remarried and is pictured here with Matt's stepmother, Antoinette.

The hardest part was enduring the hurtful comments he received from some of the workers because he was part Italian. Matt realized then that words could be powerful weapons that caused hurt as much as they could bring great joy. Seeing the power of words made him yearn that much more to be a writer. Soon he would start working to make that dream come true.

FYInfo

Lou Gehrig

In the 1920s, the New York Yankees ruled baseball, winning six pennants and three World Series. The team's most famous player was Babe Ruth, a publicity-loving party animal. But many historians have argued that possibly the greatest Yankee player ever was Ruth's teammate Lou Gehrig.

Heinrich Ludwig "Lou" Gehrig was born in New York City in 1903. His parents were German immigrants. Lou attended Columbia University to study architecture, but baseball remained his first love. So when the Yankees offered to sign Gehrig to a contract, he accepted. Both his parents had been in ill health, so Gehrig used the money he received to pay off their medical bills and send them on their first-ever vacation.

Even though Gehrig played in the shadow of the larger-than-life Babe Ruth, he quickly became one of the game's most feared hitters. In 1927, he was named the American League's Most Valuable Player, but his achievement was overshadowed when Ruth hit 60 home runs that season.

In 1933, Gehrig began to feel a mysterious weakness in his legs. He kept his concerns secret until 1938, when he began falling down and his on-field play deteriorated abruptly. On May 2, 1939, he benched himself, ending a 2,130-consecutive-game streak that would stand for over

Lou Gehrig (left) and Babe Ruth

50 years—until Cal Ripken broke the record in 1995.

Gehrig was eventually diagnosed with ALS, amyotrophic lateral sclerosis, a fatal neurological disease. On July 4, 1939, the Yankees honored the man known as the Iron Horse. An emotional Gehrig gave a short speech that began with words of gratitude for being allowed to play the game he loved. "Fans, for the past two weeks you have been reading about a bad break I got. Yet today, I consider myself the luckiest man on the face of the earth."[6]

After graduating from high school, Matt continued to play baseball—sometimes as a full-time job, and sometimes in addition to a day job. He played for company teams, including the team for the Cayuga Rock Salt Company and for the Allen-Wales Adding Machine Company.

Chapter 3

BASEBALL CALLS

Matt continued to work on the construction crew through the summer of 1934 and into the start of his senior year of high school. Even though it was hard to work and go to school at the same time, Matt knew his family needed the extra income. At the time he didn't dwell on the hardships he and his family endured, but years later Matt admitted that growing up poor made him much more determined to be a success.

"I think it probably influenced me quite a lot. I was quite young when I became quite serious about being a writer. And I thought what a great thing it would be to be a writer and help out my parents. During my summer vacation between my junior year and senior year I worked and I gave every penny except one dollar to my parents. This was my thought too, about writing—I would give them all the money until I was old enough to leave."[1]

Matt now had two passions: sports *and* writing. While he was just beginning to develop his writing skills, his athletic ability was already well honed. His on-field

Chapter 3 BASEBALL CALLS

talent caught the eye of a local semiprofessional ball club sponsored by the Cayuga Rock Salt Company. Not surprisingly, the team was called the Cayuga Rock Salts. Matt was asked to join. He accepted and became the Rock Salts' shortstop. He also continued to play on Ludlowville High's team. Being able to compete regularly sharpened Matt's skills even more, and he quickly earned a reputation as one of the area's best players.

As his high school graduation neared, Matt dreamed of attending Cornell University. He needed to take another math class to fulfill the college's admission requirements, which would mean going to summer school. It was an expense his father couldn't, or wouldn't, pay for. Frederick thought it was more important for his son to get a job than spend four more years in school.

So, instead of going to Cornell, Matt started working at the Cayuga Rock Salt Company. Fortunately for him, only older workers were sent down into the mine shafts. Since he was still a teenager, his job was safer and less physically strenuous: He picked out impurities from the salt as it moved along a conveyor belt. As he had with his earnings from the construction crew, Matt gave all but $1 of his $16 paycheck to his parents.

The bright spot of Matt's life during that time was playing baseball for the Rock Salts. Now older and stronger, Matt had developed into a solid hitter and a sure-handed fielder. His father was one of his biggest fans and supporters—although he wasn't afraid to let his son know when he played poorly. The only way to get better in a sport is to know your weaknesses and work on them.

In early 1936, Johnny Haddock, the manager of the Smiths Falls Beavers, a pro team in the Canadian-American League, saw Matt play. He got word to the Christophers that he wanted to sign Matt to a contract. What made the offer especially exciting was that the Beavers were a farm team for the mighty New York Yankees. Matt couldn't believe it.

Haddock offered Matt $75 a month, plus travel expenses for away games. Matt shrewdly asked for an extra $10 a month—and got it. The deal was official. Matt was now a professional baseball player. The time had come to see if he was really good enough to make it in the major leagues. It was also time for Matt to leave home and follow his destiny, wherever it took him.

Matt arrived by bus in Smiths Falls, Ontario, the first week of May 1936. He moved into a boardinghouse with five other players. His roommate was a pitcher from Syracuse, New York. When Matt met the rest of his teammates, he was surprised to recognize two of them! They had played on opposing teams back home. Knowing a couple of guys kept Matt from getting too homesick. He was also too busy to spend much time thinking about his family.

Matt's coach demanded that all his players make baseball their first—and only—priority, since they were being paid to play. They were expected to literally make baseball their life.

Matt's son Dale would later recount a run-in his dad had with the team manager:

> One evening he was reading a magazine in the lobby of the hotel in which they were staying. All of a sudden, the magazine was snatched out of his hands. Startled, he looked up to see his manager glaring at him.
>
> "Christopher," the manager snapped, "you're here to play baseball, eat baseball, and talk baseball. Not to read. Understand?"[2]

So that's what Matt tried to do. After his first exhibition game, he seemed to be on a fast track to the majors. A local newspaper showered him with praise:

> Starring honors were stolen neatly and completely by Matty Christopher, the dark seventeen-year-old kid who held down third base. Christy whacked in two runs with a wow of a triple, beat out a dribbler for another hit, and contributed a flashy, barehanded stop to rob Joe Mooney of a single.[3]

Chapter 3 BASEBALL CALLS

That would prove to be his one shining moment. Like many before him, though Matt was a solid player defensively, he struggled against major league–caliber pitching. (It was the same failing that made basketball star Michael Jordan quit his quest to become a pro baseball player in the 1990s.) After just two months, Matt was cut from the team for having too low a batting average. He took a bus back home, unsure what he would do next.

Not long after he returned, the manager of Brockport, another team in the Canadian-American League, contacted Matt and offered him a spot on their roster. Surprisingly, Matt declined. In his mind, the problem wasn't the team, it was his play. He didn't think he was good enough to be a pro—at least, not yet.

A short time later, Matt agreed to play with a team in the Ithaca city league. There was no money involved; it was simply a chance for Matt to play the game he loved so much. Once again, his ability made him stand out from the other players. A man named Charlie Foote offered Matt a salary to play on his Freeville-Dryden team. He accepted and went on to have his best overall season ever.

To Matt's surprise, he was a huge fan favorite. They appreciated his love of the game as much as his play on the field. One day toward the end of the season, Charlie summoned Matt out to the field before the start of the game.

"I went up to the plate and he read a letter and it was signed by about fifteen or twenty people from that area selecting me as the most valuable player of the team for that year," Matt recalled. "It was the most thrilling occasion of my life. I think I choked and almost cried. He presented me with a beautiful jacket that I wore for years. I don't know what happened to it but it probably is still around somewhere.

"Up to that point that was probably the most memorable thing in my life."[4]

Another memorable occasion was the day he was invited to play a benefit game against the New York Giants. (The team would later relocate and become the San Francisco Giants.) The game was a fundraiser for a memorial honoring John J. McGraw, the Giants' late manager.

While playing with the Freeville baseball club in 1938, Matt was voted most valuable player by members of the community. The highlight of his baseball career was getting a hit off the major league pitcher for the New York Giants during a fund-raising game.

Matt was again astounded to be recognized, this time by his peers. "I was chosen by 25 other players in central New York and most of them were college kids and I was not, to play against the New York Giants."[5]

The game took place on August 8, 1938, in McGraw's hometown of Truxton, New York. Ten thousand people filled the stands, more than Matt had ever played in front of. The highlight of the day for Matt was getting a hit off Giants pitcher Johnny Wittig.

Chapter 3   BASEBALL CALLS

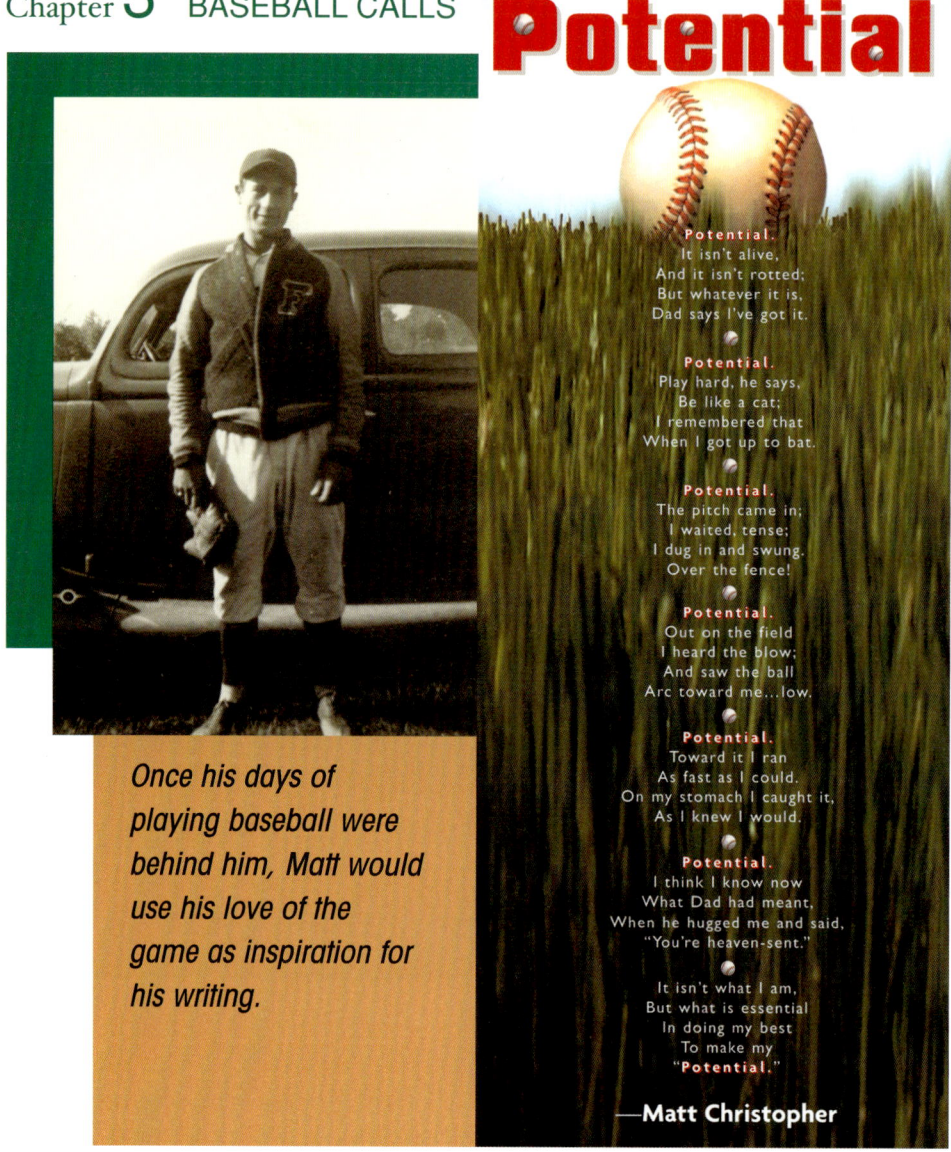

Potential

Potential.
It isn't alive,
And it isn't rotted;
But whatever it is,
Dad says I've got it.

Potential.
Play hard, he says,
Be like a cat;
I remembered that
When I got up to bat.

Potential.
The pitch came in;
I waited, tense;
I dug in and swung.
Over the fence!

Potential.
Out on the field
I heard the blow;
And saw the ball
Arc toward me...low.

Potential.
Toward it I ran
As fast as I could.
On my stomach I caught it,
As I knew I would.

Potential.
I think I know now
What Dad had meant,
When he hugged me and said,
"You're heaven-sent."

It isn't what I am,
But what is essential
In doing my best
To make my
"Potential."

—Matt Christopher

Once his days of playing baseball were behind him, Matt would use his love of the game as inspiration for his writing.

"I was thrilled, so thrilled. I was particularly happy because all 25 of us played, but I played the first five innings and I was up twice and I got one hit."[6]

Even though his team lost 8-1, the game would be one of the best memories of Matt's life. It also marked the end of his baseball dreams. Now he would single-mindedly pursue another dream: writing.

FYInfo

John J. McGraw

Known as Little Napoleon for his brusque, sometimes rude manner, John Joseph McGraw is considered one of the best managers in the history of Major League Baseball. Under his guidance, the New York Giants won ten pennants—a record for a coach—and three World Series. He was a crafty innovator and strategist of the sport, introducing the "hit and run" play and squeeze play, where the batter bunts in an attempt to let a runner on third score. He was also the first manager to hire a player as a pinch hitter and to use pitchers strictly as relievers out of the bullpen.

McGraw was born in 1873 and joined the Baltimore Orioles when he was 18. In 1893, he was named the starting third baseman and batted over .300 for the next nine years. But his talent as a player was sometimes overshadowed by his in-your-face personality. When he started managing the Giants, McGraw sometimes verbally abused his players and had frequent confrontations with umpires. He ruled his team with an iron fist and expected his orders to be followed at all times. One time McGraw fined a player $100 for missing a bunt sign—even though the player ended up hitting a home run. But McGraw also showed surprising patience with younger players and was known to help out former players financially if they fell on hard times after leaving the sport.

Autographed program

In 1932, after managing the Giants for 31 years, McGraw retired suddenly. A year later he came out of retirement to coach the National League in the first All-Star Game. That would be his last public appearance. He died February 25, 1934, at the age of 60. He was inducted into the Baseball Hall of Fame three years later.

McGraw still holds the highest lifetime batting average for a third baseman (.334) and the National League record for most wins as a coach with 2,840. Legendary manager Connie Mack, who holds the Major League record with 3,776 wins, said of McGraw, "There has been only one manager, and his name is John McGraw."[7]

Matt and Cay Christopher, 1984. A chance sighting in the park spurred a long romance between Matt and Cay. She would learn after they were married that writers need a fair amount of solitude, but Cay remained very supportive of her husband's passion— even if it meant spending most of her evenings at home alone.

Chapter 4

THE LUCKY BASEBALL BAT

While Matt was earning attention for his baseball abilities, his writing was also bringing him some notoriety. Once his father bought him the typewriter, Matt began to work diligently on stories. When he was 18, he submitted a short story to a contest sponsored by *Writer's Digest*. Matt was thrilled when he was named one of the winners. Even though the story was never printed in the magazine, that affirmation of his writing stoked Matt's hope that he would one day make a living as a writer. To make that dream come true would take much more work—and patience—than Matt could have ever imagined. But however long it took, he wouldn't spend that time alone.

A short while after winning the contest, the Christophers moved to Lansing, New York. One day Matt was outside and came across a young woman flying a kite with a boy. He stopped and watched them—not because he was a kite lover. Matt couldn't take his eyes off the teenage girl. He thought she was one of the most beautiful girls he had ever seen. He found out her name was Catherine Krupa, and they started dating.

Chapter 4 THE LUCKY BASEBALL BAT

CERTIFICATE of MERIT
awarded annually
by WRITER'S DIGEST
for distinctive ability in creative writing
TO Matthew F. Christopher

Matt submitted a short story to a contest by Writer's Digest. While his story was not published, he was awarded their certificate of merit in 1936.

Cay, as Matt called her, was still in high school, so their time together was limited to weekend nights. They dated for several years, prompting Matt's mother to urge her son to make a commitment. "You better marry that girl," she told him. "She likes you."[1]

Matt eventually took his mother's advice, and on July 13, 1940, he and Cay were married. Other than that, his life continued in its usual routine. During the day, Matt worked at an adding-machine manufacturing company. After work, he'd play ball with friends. He'd work on his writing at night, churning out short stories, plays, and even poetry. He also studied other writers' stories and enrolled in a writing class. He knew the most important thing was not to get discouraged when his stories didn't sell and to keep writing every day. Cay supported Matt's dream of being a professional writer, even though it meant spending evenings alone while her husband wrote.

In 1941, Matt read in a writing magazine that Greenburg Publishers was taking submissions for one-act plays. Those selected would be included in a published anthology, and the authors would get either a $5.00 cash prize or a copy of the book. He selected the best of his three plays, called *Escape,* and sent it in. The play was accepted and Matt chose to receive the book as his payment. It was the first time any of Matt's writing had been published, and it gave him incentive to work even harder.

At that time, there were many magazines, sometimes called pulp magazines, that ran crime stories, both true-life and fiction. Matt had always loved reading detective and crime stories and enjoyed writing them just as much.

"Determined to sell, I wrote a detective story a week for 40 weeks . . . before I sold my first story, 'The Missing Finger Points,' for $50 to *Detective Story Magazine.*"[2] Matt would later observe, "Other people could have become better writers than I am. I was just more determined to become a writer. . . . I wrote 100 detective stories before finally getting one accepted."[3]

In September 1942, Matt and Cay welcomed their first child, Martin. Becoming a father seemed to inspire Matt creatively, and he continued turning out a flood of stories. Although most were rejected, he doggedly kept writing. In late 1943, *Our Navy* magazine bought his story "The Target Downstairs" for $30, citing Matt's careful attention to detail as one of the story's strengths.

Over the next two years, Matt sold a half dozen more short stories, three of them to *Our Navy,* but his big break continued to elude him. It was hard to remain optimistic, especially with America at war. Because Matt's factory manufactured materials needed for the war effort, he was excused from having to serve in the military. While Matt was grateful that he didn't have to leave his family to go fight, he also felt guilty—especially because his brothers were soldiers. Finally, Matt decided he had to enlist. Before he could make it to boot camp, the war ended.

By 1947, Matt and Cay had three children and needed a bigger house to accommodate their family. Their new house was more expensive, adding to the difficulty they already had in trying to support three young children. Every month Cay and Matt seemed to get deeper into debt. They began to rely on the extra money Matt made writing stories, as modest as it was. Even though by this time Matt had

Chapter 4   THE LUCKY BASEBALL BAT

sold over 50 short stories, he wasn't earning anywhere near enough money at writing to consider it a true career.

After he sold his novel *Look for the Body,* Matt knew he needed to try something radically different from what he'd been doing. He still received more rejection slips than acceptances and felt as if he were in a creative rut.

He thought back to a letter he had received some time before, from a magazine editor named Delores Lehr. In it she told him, "You have a talent for writing about children . . . and children are the most difficult subjects to capture with a pen. I firmly believe that you will be selling regularly very soon. Your writing is smooth, terse, and appealing."[4]

The letter gave Matt a new sense of direction. He had never really considered writing stories specifically for children. He had nothing to lose and decided to follow Lehr's advice. Soon, his stories were being accepted by many children's magazines, such as *Teen Times, Treasure Chest,* and *Story Trails*. The money was helping Matt and Cay climb their way out of debt.

One day in late 1952, Matt was chatting with a local librarian. "After writing and selling children's sports stories to magazines, I decided to write a baseball book for children," he said. "I spoke about my idea to the branch librarian. She was immediately interested and told me that they needed sports stories badly."[5]

Her comment inspired Matt—here was a subject he knew intimately, having played sports all his life. For the first time since finishing *Look for the Body,* Matt was ready to write another full-length book. Over the long Thanksgiving weekend, instead of accompanying Cay and their children on a trip to visit relatives, Matt stayed home and wrote a sixty-page story he called *The Lucky Bat.*

In the story, a boy named Marvin wants desperately to play baseball, but no team wants him because he's a terrible hitter. Then he finds his lucky bat. It seems almost magical because it turns Marvin into an ace hitter.

Matt sent copies of his manuscript to several publishers, including Little, Brown and Company in Boston. Then, once again, he waited.

Although now best known for his sports books for young readers, Matt was a prolific writer, turning out hundreds of stories over the course of his career. He also wrote the dialogue for the Chuck White *comic strip.*

In early 1953, he received a letter from Helen L. Jones, the head of Little, Brown's children's book department. She asked if he'd be willing to rewrite part of the book and change the title to *The Lucky Baseball Bat*. Matt of course agreed—and Jones sent him a contract and an advance of $250. It was the most money he had ever made from writing—but most exciting was that Matt believed he had found his niche.

However, when he sent in his second novel, *No Baseball Allowed,* Jones politely rejected it. At first Matt was stunned and dejected. But rather than give up, he tried another idea, working hard to make the

Chapter 4   THE LUCKY BASEBALL BAT

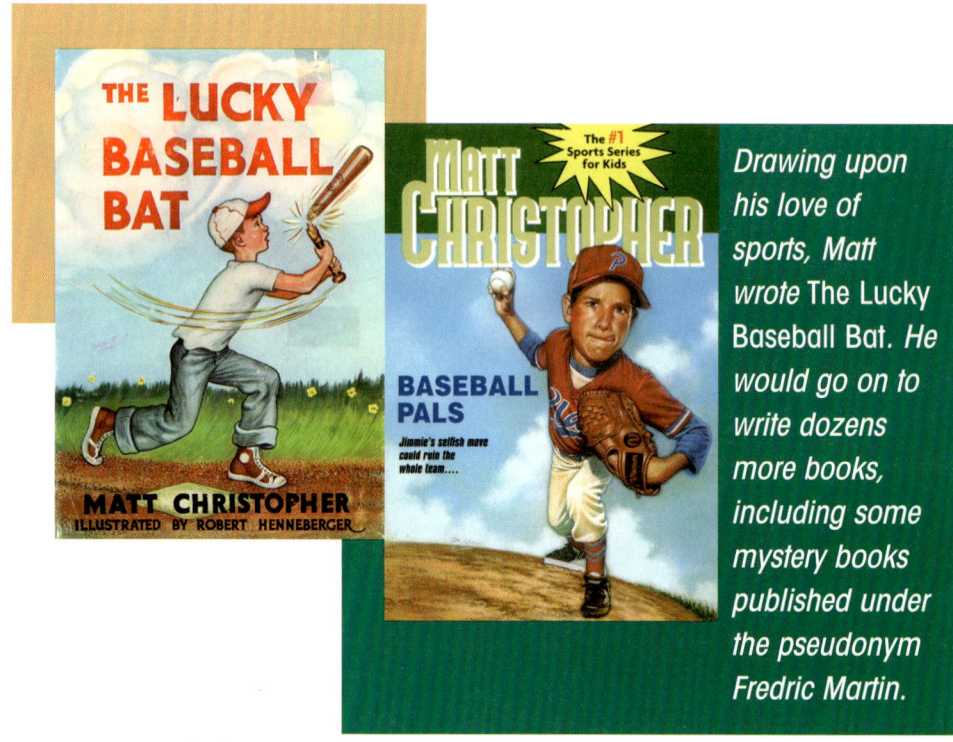

Drawing upon his love of sports, Matt wrote The Lucky Baseball Bat. *He would go on to write dozens more books, including some mystery books published under the pseudonym Fredric Martin.*

situations and characters in his book as believable as possible. He called his next novel *Baseball Pals*. It told the story of two friends, Jimmie and Paul. When Jimmie becomes captain of the team, he names himself the pitcher, even though Paul is much better. Rather than play the outfield for Jimmie's team, Paul joins another team. Jimmie eventually realizes Paul deserves to be the pitcher and must admit his mistake for the sake of the team, and their friendship.

This time, Jones quickly bought the book. *The Lucky Baseball Bat* was published in 1954, and *Baseball Pals* came out two years later. His third book, *Basketball Sparkplug*, was published in 1957 and earned Matt his first award, from the Boys Clubs of America. Finally, everything seemed to be going Matt's way. Still, now with four children to support, Matt continued working at the National Cash Register Company, which he had joined after not getting a hoped-for promotion at GE. It would be six more years before Matt felt secure enough to fulfill his lifelong dream of being a full-time writer.

FYInfo

Pulp Magazines

The late nineteenth and early twentieth centuries were a golden age for magazines. Publications at this time were printed on heavy, shiny paper that was very expensive. Magazines made this way could cost as much as a dollar, which would be the equivalent of almost $25 today.[6]

In order to make their magazines more affordable for consumers, and less expensive to produce, publishers began using a cheaper paper stock called pulp. They also began using stories from lesser-known and unknown authors and illustrators, who would accept less money than more established writers and artists.

Pulp magazines, such as *The Argosy* and *All Story,* became known for publishing "outside the box"— fiction stories that were unique or daring in their content. Another regular feature of pulp publications was the serialized story, which induced readers to come back issue after issue to see what happened next—much the way serialized TV dramas such as *24* and *Lost* hooked viewers in the early 2000s.

Author Edgar Rice Burroughs is credited with popularizing pulps. After his story "Tarzan of the Apes" was published in the October 1912 issue of *All Story,* readers began flocking to pulps. *Detective Story Magazine,* which debuted in October 1915, was the first detective pulp. In 1930, its publisher,

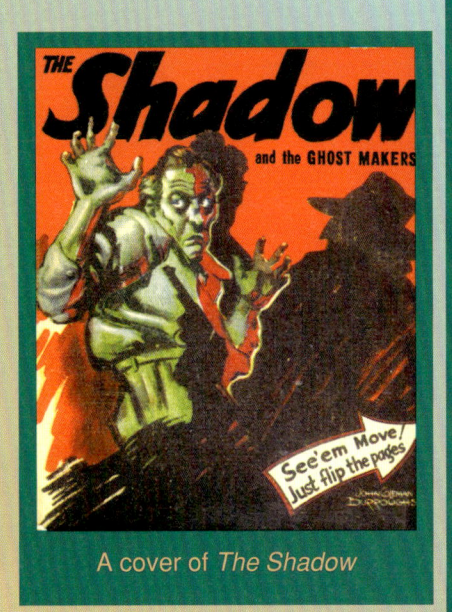

A cover of *The Shadow*

Street & Smith, sponsored a radio drama that adapted stories that had been printed in the magazine. The host of the show was known as the Shadow. The opening line of the program—"Who knows what evil lurks in the hearts of men? The Shadow knows!"[7]—became one of the best known in radio history. The character became so popular, the Shadow eventually "starred" in his own pulp, *The Shadow* magazine.

Many pulp magazines went out of business during World War II, when the government rationed the amount of paper available for what was termed nonessential publications. Their popularity further declined with the introduction of television. But the genre continues to this day in the form of mass-market paperback books referred to as pulp fiction.

Foster Caddell, who illustrated many of Matt's books, drew this picture of Matt greeting his fans in the 1960s. Matt's love of sports and special understanding of kids helped him become one of the most popular children's book authors of all time.

Chapter 5

A LASTING IMPACT

By the early 1960s, Matt Christopher was considered one of the leading authors of sports books for children. Despite his successes, he continued to work hard making sure each new book was as good as—or better than—the one before it. Matt's son Duane recalled that his dad used to write in a little room in the basement. "He'd go down there after supper and be there until midnight or one in the morning. I'd go down to kiss him goodnight and I wouldn't see him until the next morning."[1]

Matt's publisher rewarded his efforts by offering him increasingly lucrative contracts and a bigger share of sales. After so many years of struggling, Matt was now earning enough money from his books to support his family comfortably. In March 1963, he finally felt secure enough to quit his day job and become a full-time professional writer, fulfilling his childhood dream. He was 45 years old.

Matt saw each book as a new creative challenge. He recalled how as a kid, "I liked to make things—steam

Chapter 5 A LASTING IMPACT

shovels, cars, model airplanes and boats. When I was nine or ten I made a movie projector and my own film from sheets of paper. The projector never worked, but I had a great time designing and constructing it. I became a writer because I have always loved to make things starting from practically nothing."[2]

Even though he could now make his own hours, Matt approached writing like a real job and followed a strict writing schedule. "I'd get up around seven or 7:30 in the morning . . . and get to writing about nine o'clock. I would write until noon . . . and my wife would have lunch ready. About one or 1:30 I would get back to my typewriter . . . and write a couple more hours."[3]

Before Matt actually sat down to write a book, he would figure out the plot and develop the characters. "I would come up with the nucleus of the story first and then around that build my scenes." After he had all the scenes written, he said, "I put them all together and organize them. Then I would plot my story chapter by chapter. Then I set the sheets right in front of me and I start to write the story."[4]

A key element in all of Matt's books is that his characters have an obstacle to overcome or a problem to solve. "My superstars are vulnerable and have the same problems many other people have."[5]

Another characteristic of a Matt Christopher book is its believability. "I had my own personal experiences, and I saw how other players reacted to plays, to teammates' and fans' remarks and innuendoes, to managers' orders, etc. All these had a great influence on my writing. My love of the game helped a lot, too, of course. . . .

"Sports have made it possible for me to meet many people with all sorts of life stories, on and off the field, and these are grist for this writer's mill. I'm far beyond playing age now, but I manage to go to both kids' and adult games just to keep up with them, and keep them fresh in my mind. Very few things make me happier than receiving fan letters from boys and girls who write that they had never cared for reading until they started to read my books. That is just about the ultimate in writing for children. I would never trade it for another profession."[6]

Ironically, despite the success he was enjoying as a writer of sports books, Matt still longed to write mysteries. His publisher, Little, Brown, agreed to market a mystery series, but only if Matt wrote under a pseudonym. They considered the name *Matt Christopher* a brand—he was so closely associated with sports books, readers expected any book written by him to be about sports. The publisher didn't want to confuse young readers.

Matt agreed and used the name Fredric Martin—his middle and confirmation names. The first Fredric Martin book, *Mystery on Crabapple Hill,* was published in 1965. He based it on the night his grandfather had been frightened in their haunted house. The second was *The Mystery under Fugitive House.* To Matt's disappointment, neither book sold many copies, so Little, Brown declined to publish any more.

Although Matt was extremely grateful to make his living as a writer, and he enjoyed writing the sports-themed books for children, he didn't want to write *only* those kinds of books. When the editor of *Treasure Chest* magazine called in 1964 and offered him the chance to write story lines for a comic strip, Matt immediately said yes. The strip was called *Chuck White,* and Matt would write for *Treasure Chest* until the magazine went out of business in 1973.

No matter what he wrote, Matt incorporated experiences from his own life into some aspect of the stories or characters. He used two former family pets—a dog and cat named Ginger and Whitey—as the inspiration for an adventure book called *Desperate Search.* What made the story especially challenging for Matt was that the story was told from Whitey's point of view. He wrote two more adventure novels, *Earthquake!* and *Stranded.* He was particularly proud of *Stranded,* which features a blind boy and his dog who get stranded on a tropical island. Like the mystery series, none of the adventure books sold well either. Dale Christopher says his father was disappointed but reminded himself how lucky he was.

"Few authors are blessed with a talent such that everything they write sells," Matt once said. "In the long run, then, it is the persevering person who sticks with it, through thick and thin, that reaches the top rung of the writing ladder."[7]

Chapter 5 A LASTING IMPACT

While baseball remained his favorite sport, Matt recognized that young people have widely diverse interests. Wanting his books to remain relevant, he started using activities such as soccer, drag racing, and dirt biking as the backdrop of his novels.

In 1976, Cay and Matt moved to Florida to escape the harsh northern winters. Several years later, they moved again, this time to Rock Hill, South Carolina, where their son Duane lived. Although they missed the beautiful Florida weather, they enjoyed being close to their son and grandchildren. As usual, Matt spent his mornings writing—now using a computer his grandson urged him to buy. In his downtime, Matt worked in his garden, just as he had as a boy, and watched local kids play sports.

Paying attention to what kids liked helped Matt's books remain popular. In 1989, *Dirt Bike Racer* was nominated for the Maud Hart Lovelace Award, and three years later *Spy on Third Base* was nominated for the Massachusetts Children's Book Award. In 1993, Matt received the Milner Award, which is given to the favorite author of children in Atlanta.

Although Matt claimed to love all his books equally, he once admitted his favorite was *The Kid Who Only Hit Homers*. In the 1972 novel, a young boy, Sylvester Coddmyer III, is taught how to hit homers by a mysterious character named George Baruth—who the reader knows is really none other than Babe Ruth.

"It's a fantasy," Matt said, "but the main character in it could be real. . . . The only difference between a real-life boy and Sylvester Coddmyer III is the appearance of a character named George Baruth, whom only Sylvester can see and who helps Sylvester become a good ballplayer."[8] Matt liked the book so much he wrote a sequel, *Return of the Home Run Kid*.

Matt never got tired of thinking up new stories. But as he got older, his health sometimes got in the way of his writing. In 1983, he experienced a mysterious dizziness, and his doctor couldn't figure out what caused it. When it happened again two years later, Matt was diagnosed with having a bone tumor pressing against his pituitary gland. Doctors operated and removed it, but it came back six months

MATT CHRISTOPHER

Matt and Cay moved to Rock Hill, South Carolina, where Matt was treated as a celebrity. They served as Grand Marshalls for Rock Hill's Come-See-Me Parade.

later. This time he also underwent radiation treatments. Matt recovered and resumed his life of writing and spending time with his family.

In early 1997, Matt was honored with a Hero's award by the city of Rock Hill. Just a few months later, the tumor returned and he underwent his third operation. This time, he couldn't fight back. Matt died on September 20, 1997.

If there was one lesson Matt wanted all the kids who ever read one of his books to learn, it was never give up. "Don't ever stop doing what you believe. Don't ever let anyone stop you from realizing your dream."[9]

Despite his death, Matt Christopher lives on in the one way that would make him happiest—as one of the most popular children's book authors ever. To commemorate that legacy, in November 2005, his family donated a complete set of his novels to the Lansing, New York, library. They are displayed in a special case, honoring the man who never gave up, and who accomplished his dream.

FYInfo

Typewriters

It could be argued that after Gutenberg's printing press, the most important innovation for authors was the typewriter.

No individual is credited for inventing the typewriter as we know it. Many efforts were made to take the principle of movable type and apply it to a machine intended for personal use. The earliest known patent of a portable writing machine was granted in 1714 to Englishman Henry Mill, but no prototype of Mill's device exists anymore.

The biggest problem with the first generation of writing machines was that they were too heavy and cumbersome to be portable. They were also difficult to use. Finally, in 1866, a mechanical engineer named Christopher Sholes, along with colleague Carlos Glidden, invented the first practical typewriting apparatus. Although they patented their original invention in 1868, they spent an additional three years refining the machine, obtaining two additional patents. The result was the manual typewriter that we know today, equipped with a type bar and keyboard.

Originally the letters were arranged alphabetically in two rows, but using that alignment caused the keys to constantly jam. Sholes rearranged the sequence of keys so that commonly used letters were not next to each other. Not only did this help prevent jammed keys, it also allowed for faster typing. His arrangement of letters became known as the QWERTY keyboard. (Q-W-E-R-T-Y are the first six letters of the upper row of letters on a keyboard.) QWERTY keyboards remain the standard in America.

Ironically, Sholes's invention was not an instant success. But by the mid-twentieth century, typewriters had become the most widely used business tool ever—and would remain so until the introduction of another revolutionary writing machine, the personal computer.

1874 Sholes Glidden typewriter

CHRONOLOGY

1917   Born August 16 in Bath, Pennsylvania
1929   Family moves back to Portland Point, New York
1934   Matt is hired as a water boy on a road construction crew
1935   Graduates from Ludlowville High School
1936   Signs contract with Yankees farm team and moves to Smiths Falls, Ontario
1938   Plays in exhibition game against New York Giants
1940   Marries Catherine (Cay) Krupa on July 13
1941   Gets published for the first time when his play *Escape* is accepted for anthology
1942   First child, Martin, is born
1946   Daughter Pamela is born on Valentine's Day
1947   Second son, Dale, is born in May
1952   Sells first novel, *Look for the Body*
1954   *The Lucky Baseball Bat* is published
1955   Third son, Duane, is born in August
1958   Wins the Boys Club of America Junior Award
1963   Quits his day job and becomes full-time writer
1976   Moves to Florida with Cay
1983   Settles permanently in Rock Hill, South Carolina
1985   Undergoes brain surgery
1993   Wins Milner Award for favorite author of children in Atlanta
1997   Dies September 20 in Charlotte, North Carolina
2005   Matt's children donate a set of his books to library in Lansing, New York
2008   Dale Christopher tours schools with a program about his dad's life and writing

SELECTED WORKS

Books
Baseball Pals
Basketball Sparkplug
Catcher with a Glass Arm
Dirt Bike Racer
The Kid Who Only Hit Homers
The Lucky Baseball Bat
Miracle at the Plate
Penalty Shot
Red-Hot Hightops
Return of the Home Run Kid
Spy on Third Base
Touchdown for Tommy
Tough to Tackle

Short Stories
"The $100 Paper"
"No Christmas for Toby"
"Scream Your Head Off"
"Terror in the Skies"
"Twas the Day Before Christmas"
"Who's On First"

TIMELINE IN HISTORY

1876 National Baseball League is formed.
1886 Statue of Liberty is dedicated.
1888 *San Francisco Examiner* publishes "Casey at the Bat" by Ernest Thayer.
1892 Canadian PE teacher James Naismith invents basketball.
1894 Bud Hillerich patents the "Louisville Slugger" bat.
1903 The Boston Americans win first World Series.
1908 Jack Norworth writes "Take Me Out to the Ballgame."
1927 Charles Lindbergh flies nonstop from New York to Paris.
1928 Women participate in the Olympics for the first time.
1931 Severe drought hits American Plains states during the Great Depression.
1938 Author Judy Blume is born.
1941 Ted Williams bats over .400 for the season.
1947 The Maynard Midgets of Williamsport, Pennsylvania, win first Little League World Series.
1951 J.D. Salinger's *The Catcher in the Rye* is published.
1954 *Sports Illustrated* begins publication.
1989 Pete Rose is banned from baseball for gambling.
1998 *Harry Potter and the Sorcerer's Stone* is published in the United States.
2005 Cancer survivor Lance Armstrong wins seventh consecutive Tour de France.
2007 Barry Bonds beats Hank Aaron's record of 755 home runs; his record-beating baseball is branded with an asterisk to show that many believe his career has been tainted by steroid use.

CHAPTER NOTES

Chapter 1
Early Influences
1. Dale Christopher, *Behind the Desk with Matt Christopher: The #1 Sportswriter for Kids* (New York: Little, Brown, 2004), p. 12.
2. Ibid., p. 13.

Chapter 2
Humble Beginnings
1. *Good Conversations!: A Talk with Matt Christopher*, 18 minutes, Tim Podell Productions, 1994, VHS and DVD.

2. Richard D. La Guardia, "Trenton Citizens of Foreign Origin," http://www.trentonhistory.org/his/foreign.htm
3. Dale Christopher, *Behind the Desk with Matt Christopher: The #1 Sportswriter for Kids* (New York: Little, Brown, 2004), p. 14.
4. Frank Litsky, *New York Times,* "Matt Christopher, 80, Writer of Sports Novels for Children," September 27, 1997.
5. Hachette Book Group USA, "Interview: Matt Christopher,"

http://www.hachettebookgroupusa.com/authors/48/444/interview7784.html

6. Lou Gehrig's Luckiest Man Alive Speech, http://www.tommcmahon.net/2003/07/complete_text_0.html

Chapter 3
Baseball Calls

1. *Good Conversations!: A Talk with Matt Christopher,* 18 minutes, Tim Podell Productions, 1994, VHS and DVD.

2. Dale Christopher, *Behind the Desk with Matt Christopher: The #1 Sportswriter for Kids* (New York: Little, Brown, 2004), pp. 29–30.

3. Ibid., pp. 30.

4. *Good Conversations!: A Talk with Matt Christopher,* 18 minutes, Tim Podell Productions, 1994, VHS and DVD.

5. Ibid.

6. Ibid.

7. National Baseball Hall of Fame, "John J. McGraw," http://www.baseballhalloffame.org/hofers/detail.jsp?playerId=118726

Chapter 4
The Lucky Baseball Bat

1. Dale Christopher, *Behind the Desk with Matt Christopher: The #1 Sportswriter for Kids* (New York: Little, Brown, 2004), p. 38.

2. Hachette Book Group USA, "Interview: Matt Christopher," http://www.hachettebookgroupusa.com/authors/48/444/interview7784.html

3. Joe Posnanski, *York Observer,* "Writer Gives Young Readers a Wealth of Stories," November 27, 1988. http://www.mattchristopher.com/content/article.asp

4. Christopher, p. 38.

5. IPL Kidspace, "Matt Christopher," http://www.ipl.org/div/kidspace/askauthor/Christopher.html

6. MeasuringWorth.com, *Six Ways to Compute the Relative Value of a U.S. Dollar Amount, 1790–2006,* http://www.measuringworth.com/calculators/compare/index.php

7. MysteryNet.com, *The Shadow Old-time Mystery Radio Show,* http://www.mysterynet.com/shadow

Chapter 5
A Lasting Impact

1. Frank Litsky, *New York Times,* "Matt Christopher, 80, Writer of Sports Novels for Children," September 27, 1997.

2. Ibid.

3. *Good Conversations!: A Talk with Matt Christopher,* 18 minutes, Tim Podell Productions, 1994, VHS and DVD.

4. Ibid.

5. Litsky.

6. Joe Posnanski, *York Observer,* "Writer Gives Young Readers a Wealth of Stories," November 27, 1988. http://www.mattchristopher.com/content/article.asp

7. Dale Christopher, *Behind the Desk with Matt Christopher: The #1 Sportswriter for Kids* (New York: Little, Brown, 2004), p. 101.

8. Hachette Book Group USA, "Interview: Matt Christopher," http://www.hachettebookgroupusa.com/authors/48/444/interview7784.html

9. Christopher, p. 109.

FURTHER READING

For Young Adults
If you enjoyed this biography of Matt Christopher, you might also like to read about some other Classic StoryTellers in this series:

Bankston, John. *Jack London*. Hockessin, Delaware: Mitchell Lane Publishers, 2005.
Kepnes, Caroline. *Stephen Crane*. Hockessin, Delaware: Mitchell Lane Publishers, 2005.
Sherman, Josepha. *Mark Twain*. Hockessin, Delaware: Mitchell Lane Publishers, 2006.
Tracy, Kathleen. *John Steinbeck*. Hockessin, Delaware: Mitchell Lane Publishers, 2005.

Works Consulted
Christopher, Dale. *Behind the Desk with Matt Christopher: The #1 Sportswriter for Kids*. New York: Little, Brown, 2004.
Good Conversations!: A Talk with Matt Christopher. 18 minutes. Tim Podell Productions, 1994. VHS and DVD.
Hachette Book Group USA: *The Authors,* "Interview: Matt Christopher," n.d.
http://www.hachettebookgroupusa.com/authors/48/444/interview7784.html
La Guardia, Richard D. "Trenton Citizens of Foreign Origin"
http://www.trentonhistory.org/his/foreign.htm
Litsky, Frank. "Matt Christopher, 80, Writer of Sports Novels for Children." *New York Times,* September 24, 1997.
MeasuringWorth.com: *Six Ways to Compute the Relative Value of a U.S. Dollar Amount, 1790–2006*
http://www.measuringworth.com/calculators/compare/index.php
MysteryNet.com: *The Shadow Old-time Mystery Radio Show*
http://www.mysterynet.com/shadow
National Baseball Hall of Fame: *The Hall of Famers,* "John McGraw"
http://www.baseballhalloffame.org/hofers/detail.jsp?playerId=118726
Posnanski, Joe. "Writer Gives Young Readers a Wealth of Stories." *York Observer,* November 27, 1988. http://www.mattchristopher.com/content/article.asp

On the Internet
IPL Kidspace: *The Author Page,* "Matt Christopher"
http://www.ipl.org/div/kidspace/askauthor/Christopher.html
KidsReads.com: *Series Books,* "Matt Christopher"
http://aolsvc.kidsreads.aol.com/series/series-matt-christopher-author.asp
Matt Christopher—Official Web Site
http://www.mattchristopher.com
Winthrop.edu—Dacus Library
http://www.winthrop.edu/dacus/about/Archives/collections/mattchristopher.htm

GLOSSARY

apparition (aa-puh-RIH-shun)
A ghost or ghostly vision.

brusque (BRUSK)
Gruff or abrupt.

conglomerate (kon-GLOM-uh-rit)
A corporation made up of several companies specializing in different businesses.

improvise (IM-proh-vyz)
To make do with what you have at hand.

incandescent (in-kaan-DEH-sent)
Emitting visible light as a result of being heated.

innuendoes (in-yoo-EN-dohs)
Hints, suggestions.

niche (NITCH)
A place or position that is a good match for a person's talents.

pituitary gland (pih-TOO-ih-tayr-ee GLAND)
A small gland at the base of the brain that controls other glands involved in growth and maturation; sometimes called the master gland.

prototype (PROH-toh-typ)
A model or example of a new product.

quarry (KWAR-ee)
An open-pit mine from which minerals are removed.

roster (RAH-stur)
The list of players on a team.

tumor (TOO-mur)
Abnormal growth of cells that may or may not be cancerous.

INDEX

Allen-Wales team 20
Baseball Pals 34
Bath, Pennsylvania 13
Bath-Portland, Pennsylvania .. 14, 15
Burroughs, Edgar Rice 35
Brockport 24
Caddell, Foster 36
Cayuga Rock Salts 22
Christopher, Cay ... 28, 29–31, 40, 41
Christopher, Matthew
    adventure stories of 39
    awards for 34, 40, 41
    birth of 14
    cancer 40–41
    childhood 14
    children of 31, 37
    death of 41
    education of 16, 22
    family's haunted home .. 7–8, 39
    first published work 31
    jobs 8, 9, 16–17, 21–22, 34
    marries 28, 30
    most valuable player 24
    parents 13, 18
    plays baseball ... 16, 17, 20, 22–26
    pseudonym 39
    short stories of 31–32
    siblings of 14
    writes full-time 38
    writing technique 38, 39
Chuck White comic 33, 39
Cristoforo, Frederick 12, 13
Detective Story Magazine 31, 35
Edison, Thomas 11
Escape 31
Florida 40

Freeville-Dryden Team 24
Gehrig, Lou 17, 19
General Electric 9, 10, 11
Great Depression 17
Greenburg Publishers 30
Haddock, Johnny 22
Jones, Helen L. 33
Krupa, Catherine . (*see* Christopher, Cay)
Lansing, New York 29, 41
Lay the Body Anywhere 9–10
Lehr, Delores 32
Little, Brown and Company . 32–34, 39
Look for the Body 9–10, 32
Lucky Baseball Bat, The 32–33, 34
Ludlowville High School 16
Martin, Fredric 39
McGraw, John J. 25
"Missing Finger Points" 31
Mooney, Joe 23
New York Giants 24
No Baseball Allowed 33
Our Navy magazine 31
Phoenix Press 10
Portland Point 7
pulp magazines 31, 35
Smiths Falls Beavers 22
Smiths Falls, Ontario 23
South Carolina 40–41
Trenton, New Jersey 14–15
Truxton, New York 25
typewriters 17, 42
Wittig, Johnny 25
Writer's Digest 29, 30

PHOTO CREDITS: Cover, pp. 6, 12, 15, 18, 26—Dale and Duane Christopher; pp. 1, 3, 10, 20, 25, 28, 30, 33, 34, 36, 41—Louise Pettus Archives and Special Collections/Winthrop University.